The New Red Bike

Coming back from the shop he raced on ahead and waited at the gate.

"You really *can* ride your bike, can't you?" said Mum.

"Yes," said Wallace, "and now I think I'll just have a ride round the garden. Cheerio, Mum."

"Cheerio, Wallace," said Mum, and off he pedalled.

Simon Watson

The New Red Bike

and Other Stories for the Very Young

Illustrated by
Charlotte Voake

MAMMOTH

First published in Great Britain 1978
by William Heinemann Ltd
Published 1991 by Mammoth
an imprint of Mandarin Paperbacks
Michelin House, 81 Fulham Road, London SW3 6RB

Mandarin is an imprint of the Octopus Publishing Group

Text copyright © Simon Watson 1978
Illustrations copyright © William Heinemann Ltd 1978

ISBN 0 7497 0599 X

A CIP catalogue record for this title
is available from the British Library

Printed in Great Britain
by Cox & Wyman Ltd, Reading, Berkshire

Contents

The New Red Bike

When Wallace was still quite small his Grandma gave him a bicycle for Christmas.

"You'll be able to ride it when you're bigger," she said.

It wasn't brand new, the bicycle, but it was very good and bright red with silvery mudguards. It had brakes on the front *and* the back wheels. It also had stabilizers so that Wallace wouldn't fall off when he was learning to ride it.

The bicycle stayed at Grandma's house and when Wallace went to stay again he was allowed to go into the the garage and look at it. It was under an old sheet to keep it clean.

The next time Wallace went to stay Daddy got the bicycle out and fitted the stabilizers on. Wallace couldn't really ride it because his feet didn't reach both pedals at the same time. But he sat on it and Daddy pushed him round the lawn.

But the next time Wallace went to stay he *could* ride it, his feet reached both pedals when he stretched. "Look at me, Grandma!" said Wallace as he rode down the lawn.

Daddy put the bicycle on the roof-rack of the car and they drove down to the park.

There Wallace rode along the paths which were nice and hard and there was no one to bump into. Daddy walked alongside. Sometimes the bicycle started going off the path and Wallace couldn't stop it. He turned the handlebars but he turned them the wrong way and the bicycle toppled over.

"You must use the brakes," said Daddy. But Wallace couldn't work the brakes.

Wallace fell off several times altogether and got quite hurt. But he didn't mind much and he didn't cry at all because he liked his bicycle and was so proud that he could ride it.

"I rode all around the park," Wallace told Grandma when they got back.

"Well done," said Grandma. "And you didn't fall off at all?"

"Yes, sometimes," said Wallace. "But I was very brave."

"Would you like to ride it again tomorrow?" Grandma asked.

"I don't think so," said Wallace.

But now that he really could ride it Wallace was allowed to take the bicycle home. He forgot about it, though, when it was in his own garage.

One day Mummy said, "Why don't you ride your bike?" So they got it out. But the paths were too gravelly and the grass was too rough and Wallace couldn't make the bike go properly. So Mummy said, "Come on, you can ride it down the pavement to the shop."

But that wasn't any good either. It was too much

downhill and Wallace went too fast and he forgot about the brakes and caught hold of Mummy instead and nearly fell off. "Look where you're going and *steer*," Mummy said. But Wallace was frightened of falling off and he didn't like the cars and lorries going past on the road. He went too close to the houses and crashed into another bike parked against a wall.

Then he discovered the brake and used that all the time. Mummy began to get impatient. "Don't keep putting the brakes on," she said.

"But I might fall off," said Wallace.

When they were half-way back Wallace decided not to ride any further and Mum had to push his bike all the way home.

So Wallace's fine red bike began to get a bit rusty standing in a leaky garage all winter. Sometimes his baby brother Henry liked to be taken for a push round on it, but Wallace didn't want to go on it at all, even just being pushed.

Then one day Annabel came. "I got a bicycle for my birthday," she said. "I can ride it. Have *you* got a bicycle, Wallace?"

"Yes," said Wallace, "but I can't ride mine."

"Can *I* ride it?" Annabel asked.

9

"Yes, if you like," said Wallace, so Annabel's daddy got Wallace's bike out and held on while Annabel pedalled round the lawn and down the path. Wallace watched her.

"Will you do it for me?" Wallace asked Annabel's daddy.

He said, "Yes," and when Annabel had had her turn Wallace climbed on. He was a bit frightened at first but he found he could reach the pedals easily. He went all round the lawn and all round the house and he didn't fall off once.

"You said you couldn't ride your bike," said Annabel.

"Well, I can now," said Wallace.

So the next day when Mummy was going to the shops Wallace said, "I'll go on my bike shall I, Mum?"

"Yes, if you want," Mum replied.

"It's all right, you needn't hold on, Mum," said Wallace and he pedalled away down the pavement. He rode all the way to the shop and didn't once bump into anything or go off the pavement or have to cling on to Mummy.

Coming back from the shop he raced on ahead and waited at the gate.

"You really *can* ride your bike, can't you?" said Mum.

"Yes," said Wallace, "and now I think I'll just have a ride round the garden. Cheerio, Mum."

"Cheerio, Wallace," said Mum, and off he pedalled.

Finishing Breakfast

It was quite light when Wallace woke up so he got out
of bed and put his pigs in the garage. Then he went into
Mummy and Daddy's room and climbed into Daddy's
side of the bed. Daddy groaned and turned over. Wallace
clambered out to get a book and climbed back in again.
Then he wriggled off the bed to draw the curtains.

"Read me a story, Dad," he said and he sat on Daddy.

Daddy groaned again.

"Wake up, Dad," said Wallace. "Let's have breakfast,
shall we?"

Daddy pushed Wallace off and got up. They went
downstairs and Wallace let Wussy the cat in.

"What do you want for breakfast, Wallace?" Daddy
asked.

"Can I open Wussy's tin?" said Wallace.

"Yes. I said, 'What do you want for breakfast?'"

Wallace turned the handle of the tin-opener. "Corns,"
he said.

Daddy got him the Corn Flakes.

"Do you like yoghurt?" Daddy asked.

"Yes," said Wallace.

"Yes, *please*," said Daddy.

Wallace had never tasted yoghurt. He tried it with the tip of his spoon. He didn't like it.

"Can I have some milk, Dad?"

Daddy poured on some milk.

"And sugar," said Wallace. Daddy got the sugar.

Wallace tasted it again. It still wasn't nice.

"Can I have some orange, Dad?"

Daddy gave him some orange. Wallace drank a a little of it, then he began to saw at the marmalade pot with the bread-knife.

"Eat your Corns and yoghurt," said Daddy.

"I don't like it," said Wallace.

"You asked for it. Now eat it," said Daddy and he went upstairs to shave.

Wallace put on some more sugar and stirred it all up. But he still didn't like it. So he went to the cupboard and got some raisins and mixed *them* in. But he *still* didn't like it. He poured some of his orange over it and tried it again with a clean spoon. But he STILL didn't like it.

Wussy had just finished his breakfast so Wallace put his own bowl on the floor. "There you are, Wussy," he said. Wussy sniffed but he didn't like it either. He didn't even taste it.

Wallace picked up the bowl and opened the front door. He put the bowl down on the lawn. "Come on, birds," he said. "*You* have it." He ran back inside.

Daddy shouted from upstairs, "What are you doing, Wallace?" Wallace didn't answer. "Finish your breakfast," Daddy shouted.

Wallace watched through the window. One big bird flew over but it didn't notice Wallace's breakfast on the lawn. No other birds came.

Just then a sheepdog came along. Wallace ran outside. "Hey, sheepdog!" Wallace picked up the bowl and carried it to the gate. "*You* can have my breakfast." Wallace put the bowl under the gate. The sheepdog gobbled it up in no time at all. The bowl rattled on the road as his great tongue licked round it.

Wallace took the bowl back indoors and put it on the table. Then he went upstairs to his room to take the pigs out of the garage. He met Mummy coming down. Daddy shouted to him, "You finished your breakfast, Wallace?"

"His bowl's quite empty," said Mummy from downstairs.

"Good boy," said Daddy.

Wallace started singing "Old Macdonald" to his pigs.

Wallace the Policeman

In the town Wallace saw a policeman stopping the traffic. The policeman stood in the middle of the road. When he put up his hand—like this—the traffic stopped. When he waved it—like this—the traffic went on again.

"I'll be a policeman," thought Wallace.

He got home and put on his PC49 helmet and his policeman's macintosh. Then he went and stood at the front garden gate. A car came along and he stuck out his hand. "Stop!" he shouted. The car whizzed by—the driver didn't even look at him. Then the lady with the sheepdog walked by. "Stop!" shouted Wallace, holding out his hand. The lady with the sheepdog stopped.

"Why must I stop?" she said.

"Because I'm a policeman," said Wallace.

"I see," said the lady. "Can I go now?"

"Yes," said Wallace and he waved her on.

Then Wallace put out his hand as another car came by. But that one didn't stop either. "I know," said Wallace, "I should stand in the middle of the road like the policeman in the town." So Wallace undid the latch of the gate (which he wasn't allowed to do) and stepped out into the road (which he wasn't allowed to do). He looked down towards the church to see if there were any cars coming for him to stop. Suddenly there was a screech behind him—UUURRRHHHH!—and there was a huge green lorry almost on top of him. The man was angry.

He got out and shouted at Wallace, "Out of the road, you silly little sprat, unless you want to get run over." Wallace ran indoors. He didn't tell his mother that he had been in the road. The lorry stopping suddenly behind him and the man shouting had frightened him.

"It's difficult being a policeman," said Wallace to his mother.

"I expect it is," said his mother.

"What else do policemen do, Mummy?" Wallace asked.

Mummy thought. "They help people find things they've lost."

"Like my crayons?" said Wallace.

"No, bigger things than that—things like . . . well, a cat. If we lost Wussy then we'd tell the police and they might find him."

"That's a good idea," said Wallace and he ran out to find Wussy but Wussy was just coming in for something to eat. "Get lost, Wussy," said Wallace. "I'm a policeman. I'm going to find you. But don't go into the road."

But Wussy wouldn't go anywhere. So Wallace picked him up and put him outside the back door. "Go and be lost, Wussy," he said.

He waited a little while and then went out to see if he could find Wussy. But Wussy hadn't got lost at all. He was sitting on the back doorstep, washing himself.

Wallace came in again.

"What *else* do policemen do, Mum?" he asked.

"They catch burglars."

"What's a burglar?"

"Somebody who takes things that belong to somebody else."

"Like Henry when he takes my cars?"

"Not really, because he gives them back."

"You're a burglar, Henry," said Wallace and he grabbed hold of his little brother who was sitting up in his pram.

"Come on, Wallace," said his mother, "get your bike. We're going into the village."

"We might see a burglar there," said Wallace.

And they did—in the sweetshop. Wallace saw him all right. Everyone else in the shop was busy looking at things to buy and the lady behind the counter was taking in money, so only Wallace saw a man come in quietly from a door at the back of the shop, take two packets of cigarettes off the shelf and disappear back inside. The lady behind the counter hadn't seen the man at all.

"A burglar!" shouted Wallace. "Behind you!"

"What!" said the lady, looking around.

"What!" said Wallace's mother.

"What!" said all the people in the shop.

"A man came in from there and took some packets," said Wallace. "I saw him."

The lady smiled. "That's Mr Thompson," she said. "He's not a burglar. He's the owner of the shop."

"Oh!" said Wallace and the other people in the shop stared at him.

Wallace went over and looked at the fire-engine in the window. He felt a bit sad because he had been wrong about the burglar. It wasn't at all easy being a policeman.

Then a boy came into the shop and asked for a bag of marbles.

"Yes, we've got marbles," said the lady behind the counter. She came and stood by Wallace and looked amongst the toys for the marbles. "I'm sure we've got some *somewhere*," she said. "But I can't see them at the moment."

Wallace said, "I'll find them for you." And he looked too. Soon he found them. They were in a very difficult place, underneath a packet of balloons so that you could hardly see them.

"Thank you," said the lady. "I'd never have found them there. What a clever policeman you are!"

Wallace and his mother left the shop.

"It's not *so* difficult being a policeman," said Wallace,

as he pedalled along on his bicycle. "Stop!" he shouted as a car went past. But it didn't stop. Nor did two lorries, even though he stuck his arm right out and shouted as loud as he could.

When he got home Wallace took off his coat and his helmet and hung them up.

"I don't think I'll be a policeman when I grow up," he said. "I don't like stopping the traffic."

"But you're good at finding things," said his mother.

"Yes," said Wallace. "I found the marbles for the lady in the shop, didn't I?"

"You did."

"I know what," said Wallace. "I won't be a traffic policeman. I'll be a *finding* policeman . . . that's what I'll be."

The Sandpit

Daddy came home one day with a huge sort of box on the roof-rack.

"What's that?" Wallace asked.

"That," said Daddy, "is your new sandpit."

It was so big Daddy could hardly lift it by himself. It was heavy wood and painted blue. Standing on its side it was as tall as Wallace. Daddy put it in a corner of the yard.

"What do you think of that?" he said.

"Smashing," said Wallace, "but we haven't got any sand."

"We'll go and get some," said Daddy.

Daddy and Wallace put on their working clothes and Wallace rode in the wheelbarrow all the way to the builder's in the village. Daddy shovelled in lots of clean dry sand. Wallace felt it run through his fingers.

"What a lot of sand!" he said as he helped Daddy wheel the barrow home.

"It *is* a lot," said Daddy. "Phew! my back. This is a heavy load. I hope it'll last you the summer, Wallace. Don't go wasting it, will you?"

"I won't," said Wallace.

When they got home Daddy tipped the barrow up and all the sand whooshed down into the pit.

"It's just like a tipper," said Wallace and he jumped with both feet into the pile. "*So much!*" he said. Then he went in to collect everything he'd need: his bucket and spade, his tractor and trailer, all his lorries, Henry's baby plastic cups and one of Mummy's wooden spoons.

Wallace poured the sand like water out of his bucket. He threw spadefuls of it up into the air and watched it falling in a shower. But the sand was too dry to shape into anything so Mummy gave him some water. He made roads and tunnels. He made an underground car park. He buried the fork-lifter and almost couldn't find it again. He took loads off to the flower-pot for mixing into cement. Then Henry came and sat in the corner of the pit, eating the sand.

Wallace went in for tea.

"Don't waste all the sand, will you, Wallace?" said Mummy.

"I won't," said Wallace.

When he went out again he looked at his sandpit and

said, "Oh no!" Wussy had used the sandpit as a lavatory and Daddy had to get his trowel and take the mess away.

"I'll have to make a cover for the sandpit," said Daddy.

Wallace got to work again. He fetched his aeroplane and loaded that and flew sand off to the flower-bed. It took lots of journeys to get enough to cover one of the flowers because the aeroplane dropped it on the way.

Then Wallace took his big tipper-truck road-mending in the yard. There were a lot of holes to be filled in. Wallace tipped sand into the holes and smoothed them over with his spade.

Then it started to rain. Wallace ran to Daddy.

"Daddy, have you made the cover for the sandpit?"

"Not yet," said Daddy. "Give me a chance!"

"My sand'll get wet," said Wallace.

"Never mind," said Daddy. "It's only a shower."

While it rained Wallace stood on a box and looked out of the tool-shed window. Daddy was finding some wood to make a cover.

When the rain stopped they both went out to the sandpit.

"Oh goodness!" said Wallace when he saw it. "*Where's* all the sand gone?" There was hardly any left in the pit. It had spilt over the sides, it was all over the ground and it was in the flower-pot. But in the sandpit there were just a few little piles.

"*And* it's in the flower-bed," said Daddy angrily. "You *have* wasted it, Wallace. You've wasted it all. All that sand gone in one afternoon."

"Sorry, Daddy," said Wallace. "Will you get me some more?"

"Certainly not!" Daddy said.

Wallace went inside.

"Take your boots off," said Mummy. "Carefully. I expect they're full of sand too." And they were. Wallace turned his boots upside down over a cup. The sand from his boots almost filled the cup.

"I didn't waste it *all*, did I?" said Wallace. "Daddy *will* buy me some more sand, won't he, Mummy?"

"He *might*," said Mummy. "Perhaps he will if you go and clear up some of the sand you've spilled."

"All right," said Wallace.

Wallace took the cupful of sand from his boots and emptied it into the pit. He dug out some of the sand he'd filled the holes in the yard with. He got some out of the flower-pot and quite a lot out of the flower-bed. It was all very wet and there was a lot of brown earth mixed up in the sand as well. But it was something.

"Daddy, I haven't wasted it *all*, have I?" he said.

Daddy smiled. "No, not quite all," he said.

"*Will* you buy me a bit more then?" Wallace asked.

"Oh! all right," said Daddy. "But no more wasting now."

Wallace jumped into the wheelbarrow. "Come on then," he said. "Let's go."

And off they went back to the builder's for another load of sand.

The Tortoise With a Name Shirt

One day Wallace's Grandma came to see him.

"I've brought you a present," she said.

Wallace hoped it was a tortoise because that was what he had been asking everybody for. But Grandma brought out a paper bag that couldn't possibly have a tortoise in it. Wallace was disappointed. But when he opened the bag he found something nice all the same; it was a T-shirt, but not just an ordinary T-shirt.

"Look on the other side," said Grandma.

Wallace turned the shirt over and there was a row of soldiers and under each soldier was a letter. Wallace saw a W then an A . . .

"There now, Wallace," said Grandma. "What does that say?"

"Wallace!"

There it was—WALLACE—written in big black letters under the soldiers.

"Why don't you put it on and give Mummy a surprise?" said Grandma.

So Wallace took off his old shirt and put on his new one.

"It's my name shirt," he said. He couldn't see his name or the soldiers very well when he had the shirt on, but he could feel them because they felt different from the rest of the shirt. Wallace ran to Mummy.

"Hello, Mum. Do you know what my name is?" he asked. Mummy had her back to him so she couldn't see his new shirt. She said, "Well, of course I know what your name is—it's . . ." Then she turned round and saw the shirt. "It's WALLACE!" she called out. "My goodness, what a lovely shirt!"

"Now everyone will know who I am," said Wallace. And they went to the shop to get some biscuits for tea.

"Well, hello Wallace," said the man. "That's a nice shirt."

"Yes," said Wallace. "It's my name shirt."

"Umm—very useful too," said the man. "If you got lost people could easily find you. Even if they didn't know your name they'd know who you were, wouldn't they, just by looking at your shirt?"

"Yes, they'd soon find me," said Wallace.

The next day Mummy took Wallace and his brother Henry in the pushchair to town.

There were so many people in the market and Mummy was so busy with Henry and the shopping that Wallace got left behind. Mummy was just putting the apples in her bag when she turned and looked and Wallace wasn't there.

"Oh, gracious!" thought Mum. "Where *has* he got to? I know—he's probably gone to the toy stall." So she went there.

"Yes, there *was* a soldier-boy with Wallace on his shirt," said the man at the toy stall. "He was trying to ride the tractor-and-trailer so I said, 'Wallace, is your Mum giving you that for your birthday?' and he said, 'No, she's giving me a tortoise.' So I said, 'You'd better not ride that tractor then.' And off he went. That's a good idea, I thought, having his name on his front. Folks'll know who he is and he won't get lost."

"Well, I've lost him," said Mum.

"Did you say a boy with 'Wallace' on his T-shirt?" another lady said. "Lost, is he? I saw him just a minute ago—down that way—by the pet stall."

"Thank you," said Mum and off she went again. And there was Wallace looking at the animals at the pet stall.

"Wallace! I thought I'd never find you," said Mum.

"But you did, didn't you, Mum? Because I had my

name shirt on and everybody knew I was Wallace."

"That's right," said Mum. "Now stay with me this time."

On the way home Wallace said, "When I have my tortoise how am I going to keep that from getting lost?"

"Perhaps it could have a label round its neck," said Mum.

"It might tread on a label though," said Wallace. "*I* know what we could do: we could write the tortoise's name on its shell with my felt pens and that would be the same as a name shirt, wouldn't it?"

"What a good idea!" said Mummy. "In red perhaps."

"Yes, red," said Wallace. "But I haven't got a tortoise yet, have I, Mum?"

"Don't worry," said Mum. "You will have soon. And what are you going to call it?"

"Roy," said Wallace.

On his birthday Mum said, "Come on outside, Wallace. I've got a present for you there."

They went out on to the lawn.

"Now I wonder where it's got to," said Mum. "It was here a minute ago."

Just then Wallace spotted something red on the ground amongst the flowers nearby. Something red? It was the letter O. Wallace looked closer and there was an R and a Y. ROY. Wallace picked up his tortoise.

"Here he is, Mum," he said. "I've found him." Wallace stroked his tortoise's back. "Don't worry, Roy," he said, "you won't get lost, not with your name shirt on."

Wallace and the Jerbils

One day a lady and a little girl brought some jerbils to stay at Wallace's house.

The jerbils lived in a glass fish tank, which was very heavy. The tank had a lid made of wood and wire netting.

"That's so they can't get out," said Daddy.

"What would happen if they *did* get out?" asked Wallace.

"I expect Wussy would catch them and eat them," said Daddy.

They put the jerbils' tank on the toy box in the sitting-room. Wussy the cat jumped up and sniffed at the tank. Then he climbed on to the wire-netting lid and sat on it looking down at the jerbils.

"Go away, Wussy," said Wallace fiercely. "You can't eat them." And he shoved Wussy off.

The jerbils had made a nice fluffy nest out of chewed-up cardboard. They had a piece of wood to run along and sharpen their claws on. And they had two little tins in the corner, one for food and the other for water.

"It's a nice house," said Wallace. "Can I feed them now?"

He took the packet of food and poured some into their tin. They had peanuts and broken dog-biscuit and sunflower seeds. And Wallace gave them half a carrot as well.

"That should keep them going for the night," said Daddy.

The two jerbils held nuts in their front paws and sat up on their hind legs to eat them. They ran about and scrabbled at the glass sides of the tank as if they wanted to get out.

"You stay in there," said Wallace. And then it was time for him to go to bed.

In the morning he ran downstairs to see the jerbils. But at first he *couldn't* see them in their tank. "Jerbils, where are you?" he said. The fluffy nest of chewed-up cardboard began to shake and one of the jerbils stuck his nose out and twitched his whiskers.

"*There* you are!" said Wallace. "Have some breakfast."

Wallace took their lid off and gave them some more of their food. "Would you like some Weetabix?" he said. He went into the kitchen to get some. Then Daddy came down and let in Wussy and they opened Wussy's tin and they ate some Puffed Wheat.

"Have you fed the jerbils, Wallace?" Daddy asked.

"I was just doing that," said Wallace and he went in to take the jerbils some Weetabix. But he soon came running back into the kitchen. "Daddy! Daddy!" he said, "the jerbils have gone!"

"Oh no!" said Daddy and they both dashed in to look.

"Perhaps they're in the nest," said Daddy and he poked his finger into the fluff. But both the jerbils had gone. "Oh dear! Quickly, Wallace. We must find them before they get away."

"We must find them before Wussy catches them," said Wallace. "Find Wussy!"

"Find the jerbils!" said Daddy.

Then they both got on their hands and knees and hunted round. Wallace looked inside his garage. Daddy looked in the fireplace.

Wallace went into the kitchen and looked in the rubbish bin. He tried to look under the stove but it was too dark.

Daddy looked among the boots in the boot room. He looked behind the flour-bag in the store-room.

"Do you think the jerbils are in the garden, Daddy?" asked Wallace. "Shall I have a look?" And he went to the door.

"Don't open the door!" Daddy shouted. "If they get outside we'll never find them. Keep looking inside the house, Wallace."

So they went on looking.

"Do you think they've gone upstairs?" said Wallace.

"I don't think they *could* climb upstairs," said Daddy. "They're too small."

"Perhaps Wussy's eaten them already," said Wallace.

Then Daddy suddenly said, "Here they are!" And there they were under an arm-chair in the sitting-room, hidden by the covers. They were nibbling at an old peppermint that Wallace had left there.

"Come, on jerbils," said Wallace, and he made pussy noises at them. But they went on nibbling. Then Daddy reached out his long arm and grabbed one of them and put it back in its tank and plonked the lid on. That jerbil still had the peppermint and he was still nibbling at it.

"Well, that's one," said Daddy. "Now where's the other?"

"He ran behind the bookcase," said Wallace.

"That's awkward," said Daddy. "I can't reach him there. I tell you what: you go one end, Wallace, and poke at him with a ruler and I'll catch him when he comes running out the other end."

Wallace took the ruler and looked behind the bookcase.

"Can you see him?" said Daddy.

"No," said Wallace.

"Well, wave the ruler anyhow," said Daddy. He bent down at the other end, ready to pounce.

Wallace stuck the ruler in behind the bookcase and wiggled it about. Then he heard a loud "Ouch!" from Daddy.

"Have you got him?" asked Wallace.

"Yes," said Daddy, and he rushed the second jerbil back to the tank. "But he got me too," he said. And Daddy showed Wallace some teeth marks in his hand where the jerbil had bitten him. "A nasty little nip," said Daddy. "And now, Wallace, remember: if you take the lid off you mustn't go away."

"Yes, Dad."

Both the jerbils were back at the peppermint again.

Daddy put the lid firmly on the tank and Wallace put one of his heaviest lorries on top of the lid in case Wussy should try to nudge it off.

"Well, I wonder where Wussy is after all that," said Daddy.

Wallace found him. He was fast asleep in the airing cupboard.

New Shoes

Wallace and his mother went to town.

"We're going to get some new shoes for me, aren't we, Mummy?" said Wallace.

"That's right," said Mummy, "smart new shoes. Not for playing in the sandpit."

"That's right," said Wallace, "*smart* new shoes."

The lady in the shop said, "What size is he?"

"Size seven, I should think," said Wallace's mother.

The lady measured Wallace's foot.

"Good heavens!" she said. "He's size nine!"

"Good heavens!" said Wallace's mother. "Size nine!"

"I'm size nine," said Wallace.

The lady brought some size nine shoes. They looked very big. There were blue ones and brown ones and black ones. Some were clumpy ones and some were sandals. Some you slipped on and some you buckled on.

They chose a pair of blue sandals. The sandals had a pattern of holes like leaves so that Wallace could see his socks through the top. They had straps and little buckles that tinkled in a nice way. The bottoms of the shoes were still clean and white because they hadn't been worn.

The sandals smelt good. "That's leather," said Wallace's mother.

Wallace was allowed to go out of the shop wearing his new shoes. His old shoes were in Mummy's basket.

"We don't need them any more, do we, Mummy?"

"Someone might," said Mummy.

In the car park Wallace stepped in a puddle by mistake. It splashed his new sandals. "Mummy!" said Wallace.

"You must mind where you're going when you're wearing smart things," said Mummy.

"I can show my new shoes to Vincent when he comes to play, can't I, Mummy?"

"Yes, but you mustn't go into the sandpit with them."

In the afternoon Vincent came to play.

"Mummy," said Wallace, "Vincent has brought his digger-and-trencher."

"Good," said Mummy and she went inside because the telephone was ringing.

Wallace and Vincent worked the digger-and-trencher in the sandpit. There was a lot of loading and unloading to do. They were making roads.

"We need some cement," said Vincent.

Wallace got his watering-can and began to mix. They made a cement park for the digger-and-trencher and a cement road for the lorries.

"And we need some earth too," said Vincent.

Wallace got his bucket and spade and began to dig earth out of the flower-bed. He found a worm so he dug a big hole and put the worm in and filled the hole with water. The worm disappeared. Vincent brought the digger over to fill up the hole.

Then Mummy came out. "Wallace!" she shouted. She was very angry. "What did I tell you? *Look* at your new shoes!"

Wallace's smart new blue sandals didn't look smart and new at all. They were sopping wet and covered with sand and earth. One of them had even had some of its blue scraped off. His new sandals looked almost as old as his old ones.

Wallace's mother took them off in a rather rough way. "They'll have to be wiped clean," she said, "and dried and polished again. Now put your boots on."

"Can't I wear them any more today?" Wallace asked.

"No, you'll be lucky if you *ever* wear them again. You've almost ruined them."

Wallace began to cry.

When he was being dried after his bath that night he said, "Can I sleep with my new shoes by my bed?"

"They're downstairs, drying," said his mother.

"I *will* be able to wear them tomorrow, won't I?" asked Wallace.

"I don't know," said his mother. "I'm not sure you deserve to."

Wallace was very sad. He climbed into bed and didn't say anything. His mother kissed him goodnight.

"If you're good you can wear them," she said. "But *not* in the sandpit."

"No," said Wallace.

"You mustn't wear them outside *at all*."

"All right."

Wallace went to sleep. He woke up in the morning and thought of his new shoes. He wondered if they would be dry yet. He decided to go downstairs and have a look. But as he jumped out of bed, there they were, side by side, on the floor next to his slippers. He *had* slept with his new shoes by his bed after all. They were quite dry and quite clean and quite blue and even the bottoms were almost white again. And they still had that nice leather smell.

Wallace put them on and ran into his parents' room.

"Mummy!" he said. "My new shoes are *new* again!"

The Pill Box

"Road works!" Wallace called out as they drove along to nursery school. "It was the men-at-work sign, Mum."

"I wonder what they're doing," said Mum.

But when they got to the cross-roads they could see bulldozers and diggers clearing the bank away.

"They're straightening the road," said Mum, "so that cars can see other cars coming at the cross-roads."

"Then they won't crash into each other," said Wallace.

"That's right," said Mum.

And then they followed a lorry taking sandy earth from the cross-roads.

"I wonder where they're taking it," said Wallace.

Soon the lorry stopped just the other side of the railway bridge. It dumped the sand and a digger shoved it down on to the railway line.

"The railway doesn't run any more," said Mum, "so they're filling it up with rubbish."

The next day when they came to the cross-roads Wallace said, "Look, Mum, how much sand they've taken away. But what's that thing?"

He pointed to a funny-looking brick building, rather low and with no windows, only a dark slit in the side.

It was now standing all by itself in the middle of the bit the diggers were clearing.

"It's a pill box," said Mum.

"A pill box?"

"It's a place for soldiers to shoot their guns from," said Mummy. "So it's very strong. I shouldn't think those diggers will be able to move it."

"I wonder what they'll do then," said Wallace.

The next day the pill box was still there and the diggers were moving more earth away so that the pill box stuck up even more by itself. They could see its foundations.

"I expect they'll have to get a crane," said Wallace, "and lift it all up in one piece and drop it into the sea."

On the third day the pill box was still there, but not all of it. Bits had been nibbled out of the top and they could see how *that* had been done for as they waited at the cross-roads the pneumatic drill man got up on to the top of the pill box and—da-da-da-da-da—started drilling away.

"That's how they're doing it, Mum," said Wallace, "with a pneumatic drill."

And when they came back at lunch time even more of the pill box was crumbled away so that it no longer had the shape of a cake but the shape of an old ruin. Bits of thick wire were sticking out of the concrete; they were bent and tangled.

"Those are the reinforcements," said Mum, "to make the concrete stronger."

"It's not strong enough, though, is it?" said Wallace. "The drill's breaking it down."

As they drove up to the cross-roads the next morning

Wallace said, "I wonder how the drill man is getting on with the pill box."

When they got to the cross-roads Wallace cried out, "Mum—it's gone—the pill box is all gone!" There was nothing left except a few bricks on the sand.

"Well, that's it," said Mum. "We've seen the last of the pill box."

"I suppose they've pushed it down into the railway," said Wallace, "with the other earth."

"I expect so," said Mum.

But as they came round a corner further along the road they had to stop suddenly because the narrow road was blocked by two lorries trying to pass. The one coming towards them was a lemonade lorry and the one ahead of them was a . . .

"Look, Mum!" Wallace cried out, "that lorry has got the pill box on it."

And there, on the lorry just in front of them, were great chunks of the pill box with bits of the rusty reinforcing-wire sticking out.

"Now we'll be able to see if it *is* going to the railway," said Wallace.

So they followed it and it was. It pulled into the side just over the bridge.

"Ooh! Can we watch, Mum?" said Wallace.

"All right," said Mum, "just for a minute."

So they stopped too and got out and watched the lorry's back tipping up slowly and the bits of pill box come rumbling out. Then the digger came along and Wallace looked over the bridge as the pill box went crashing down to the bottom.

In a few weeks the sandy earth at the cross-roads was covered over with tarmac and cars could go along safely. But each time Wallace and his mother stopped at the cross-roads on their way to nursery school, Wallace would say, "That's where the pill box used to be, isn't it, Mum?"

Chicken Feathers

One day Wallace went into the tool-shed to get a trowel. Inside the tool-shed there was something enormous and white hanging on the wall. It was a great big bird.

Wallace ran out of the tool-shed and went into the house.

"Mummy, there's an enormous white bird in the tool-shed."

"Yes," said Mummy, "it's a chicken."

"It won't hurt me, will it?" said Wallace.

"No," said Mummy, "it's dead."

Wallace ran back to the tool-shed. He opened the door a bit and then he shut it again. Then he opened it and looked at the bird from outside the shed. The bird's yellow feet were tied together with string and the string was hung on a hook. Its head hung down with its beak pointing down. Its eyes were half closed as if it were just going to sleep. Wallace wanted to touch it but he was frightened to.

He ran back into the house again.

"It can't see me, can it, Mum?" he said.

"No," said Mum, "because it's dead."

"What's it for?" Wallace asked.

"It's for eating," said Mummy. "We're going to have it for lunch tomorrow."

"How can we eat it?" said Wallace. "It's covered in feathers."

"Daddy's going to pluck it this evening," Mummy said. "He's going to take the feathers off. Perhaps you can help him."

Wallace ran back to the tool-shed. He wanted to try and pluck the chicken but he didn't want to get too close to it. He didn't like the look of its beak. So he got a stick and tapped its neck. The chicken seemed to come alive. It wobbled and the beak swung to and fro as if it were pecking. Wallace ran away.

When Daddy came home Wallace watched him take the chicken down from its hook. He held it by its yellow feet and its head knocked against his legs as he walked but he didn't seem to notice.

"It's dead, isn't it, Dad?" said Wallace.

"Yes," said Daddy. Daddy dropped the chicken into a large cardboard box outside the kitchen door. It made a feathery kind of thump as it fell in and its beak scratched against the side of the box. Daddy went into the kitchen.

Wallace looked at the chicken. He just touched one of its dirty claws with the tip of his finger. "I'll touch its feathers too," he thought, and he was just putting his hand in when he kicked the box and the chicken's head suddenly fell to one side and Wallace jumped.

Daddy came back wearing an apron and carrying a chair.

"It came alive a bit then," said Wallace.

Daddy picked it up and started tearing feathers off. They floated down into the box and one or two blew away on the wind. Soon there was quite a soft bed in the bottom of the box. Wallace laid his hand on the feathers. "It's like a nest," he said. There was a bare patch on the bird and it looked pink and white.

"Nice and plump," said Daddy.

"I don't want to have it for lunch," said Wallace.

Then it was time for bed. "Mummy, I don't want to eat the chicken," he said.

"You don't have to," Mummy replied.

The next day at lunch Daddy carved the chicken. Its beak had gone but it still had its legs. It smelled delicious and there was gravy.

"I don't want any chicken," said Wallace.

"Have some potatoes and gravy then," said Mummy.

But the gravy was good and the potatoes were good and Wallace had a little bit of meat because he liked meat and that tasted good and he asked for some more and he ate all that too.

When they had all had enough Daddy said, "That was delicious."

"Yesterday it was hanging in the tool-shed," said Wallace. "And you plucked it, didn't you, Daddy?"

After lunch Wallace found the cardboard box. It was half full of fine white feathers. Wallace buried his hand in them. The feathers were so soft he could hardly feel them. Then he lifted out a handful and threw them up in the air and some of them came down again like snow and some went up and up and disappeared out of sight into the sky.

A Ride With the Builders

One morning some builders arrived in a blue van. The van had an open back.

One of the builders let down the side with a clatter. Then he jumped up on to the back and started unloading some planks and long metal poles.

"What's all that?" asked Wallace, as the men unloaded.

"Scaffolding," said the big man.

"What's it for?"

"It's for taking the roof off."

The men carried the scaffolding round to the back of the house and started putting it together. They dug holes in the lawn for two of the poles. Then they spannered the other poles together in a frame and put the planks up so that they could walk high up by the roof.

Then they started taking the tiles off the roof and stacking them on the planks.

"What are you taking the roof to bits for?" asked Wallace.

"To put lining on and keep you warm inside," said the big builder. "Look how the sparrows have been in." He threw down a handful of hay. "That's a nest," he said. "Would you like to come up and have a look?"

"Yes please," said Wallace. So the builder came down and asked Wallace's mummy if Wallace might go up onto the roof. She said yes and Wallace climbed all the way up the tall ladder with the builder behind him. Wallace clung on at the top because it was so high. He could see much further than when he was up his tree on the lawn. He could see houses miles away. But it made him feel a bit odd and the builder helped him down again.

The men threw down more nests. Then they started throwing down bits of plaster and broken tile and little strips of wood.

"Best mind out now," said the builder. "You don't want this on your head."

"Or my foot," said Wallace.

Then the big builder came down and started collecting rubble in his wheelbarrow.

"Can I help?" asked Wallace. "I've got a wheel-barrow."

"Come on then," said the builder.

Wallace brought his barrow. It was green with red handles and it had two wheels with rubber tyres.

Wallace and the builder filled their barrows with rubble and took them to a heap under the lilac tree.

"What will we do with this?" asked Wallace.

"Perhaps your dad could make a path with it," said the builder.

"Perhaps a tipper-truck could come and take it away," said Wallace.

Then the big builder took his barrow to the van to fetch the rolls of lining.

"Can *I* get up onto the back?" asked Wallace.

The big builder lifted him up. There were all sorts of things there: ladders and buckets and spades and rope and sand. There was a bar across the top of the cab for tying ladders to and Wallace held on to that pretending the van was going along.

"Would you like a ride?" said the big builder.

"Yes, *please*," said Wallace.

Mummy said he could and she would collect him from the builders' yard. So after tea the builders packed up for the day and Wallace was lifted into the back of the

van with all the tools and things. The big builder got alongside him and one of the other builders started up the van.

Off they went with a bit of a jerk. Wallace clung on to the bar across the top of the cab and the builder stood right beside him, not holding him but ready to catch him if he should fall.

They whizzed along and the air blew into Wallace's face and through his hair. It felt funny being out of doors like walking but going fast like driving.

"Did you see that?" said the builder as they went along, and he pointed to a broken down bit of wall beside the road.

"Yes," said Wallace.

"A fire-engine did that," said the builder. "It was turning round so fast it didn't have time to look where it was going. It hit the wall and knocked it over."

Just as the builder said that, a cat ran out into the road, the driver of their van swerved suddenly and Wallace stumbled sideways and would have fallen over amongst the sand and buckets if the builder hadn't caught him.

"That was a close one," said the builder.

"Yes," said Wallace. "We nearly went through the wall like the fire-engine."

Soon they were at the yard.

"Would you like to see the circular saw?" the big builder asked.

There it was in the shed: an enormous round metal thing on a stand, as big as a car tyre, with sharp teeth.

The builder pressed a button and the saw whirled round and round. Then he got a long piece of wood and laid its end into the saw. The saw started making a terrible loud tearing, screeching noise so that Wallace had to cover his ears. Sawdust flew out as the big long plank was cut into two.

"That's good," said Wallace when the engine was turned off.

"You can have some of these little sawn-off bits of wood if you like," the builder said.

"Ooh, yes!" said Wallace. "They'd be good for bricks. Thank you."

Then Mummy arrived to take him home and when they got there Daddy was walking about on the scaffolding.

"*I've* been up there, Dad," said Wallace.

"Have you?" said Dad. "It's very high."

"*And* I went in the builders' van and we nearly had an accident," said Wallace.

"Good gracious!" said Dad. "And what have you got in that bag?"

"Bricks," said Wallace, and he went inside to play with them. He built them into an enormous wall and then—CRASH—he drove his fire-engine into them at top speed and sent them flying all over the floor.

Wallace for Sale

Mummy and Wallace were coming back from the shops.

"Can I have my lolly now, Mum?" asked Wallace.

"No," said Mummy. "It's nearly lunch time. You can have it after lunch."

"I want it now," said Wallace.

"Well, you can't have it," said Mummy.

When they got home Mummy asked Wallace if he wanted sausages or a beefburger for lunch.

"Sausages," said Wallace.

Then Mummy made his brother Henry's lunch and Wallace said, "Can I have my lolly now?"

"No," said Mummy. "After lunch, I told you."

"Don't *want* any lunch," said Wallace.

"No lunch, no lolly," Mummy replied. "Do some drawing for a while."

Wallace scribbled all over his paper and dug a hole in it with his pencil.

"Is my lunch ready?" he asked.

"Not yet. Be patient. Why don't you do your Lego?"

Wallace lay on the bench and kicked his box of Lego so that the pieces spilt all over the floor.

"You're tired," said Mummy, "that's your trouble."

"I'm not," said Wallace.

"Here are your sausages anyway."

"I don't *want* sausages. I want my lolly."

"You know what I said," Mummy answered.

Henry was sitting on the floor, drinking out of his bottle. Mummy wasn't looking so Wallace took the bottle out of his mouth and threw it under the table. Henry began to cry.

"What have you done to him?" said Mummy, coming back in.

"Nothing," said Wallace.

"Eat up your sausages."

"Don't *want* them," said Wallace and he shoved his plate so hard across the table that one of the sausages rolled off and landed on the floor.

"Right! That's it!" said Mummy. "Upstairs. Go on! Upstairs! Upstairs until you can behave."

Wallace began to cry as Mummy bundled him up the stairs into his room.

"You can come down when you're going to be nice," said Mummy.

"No!" shouted Wallace and he lay on the floor and kicked around so that his farm went flying.

And he cried and he cried. And then after a while his crying noise became more like a tractor noise and soon Wallace was loading up straw bales to carry off to the pig-sty.

"Are you ready to be nice?" Mummy shouted up the stairs.

Wallace began to cry again. "Yes," he said, and came down the stairs.

"Would you like to hear a story?" said Mummy.

"Yes," said Wallace and he came and sat on Mummy's

49

lap. Henry was under the table now. He was eating the sausage that Wallace had knocked on to the floor and he had his bottle in the other hand. He was very happy.

Wallace was feeling a bit hungry now too and Mummy fed him his lunch off his plate like a baby. Wallace liked that.

"What's the story?" he said.

"Once there was a boy who nagged his mother all the time about wanting an ice lolly. 'Mummy, can I have a lolly?' he said all day long. Even when he'd just had one he'd say, 'Mummy, can I have another one?' He wouldn't eat anything else at all—"

"Like me," said Wallace.

"Like you," said Mummy. "He wouldn't play. He was nasty to his little brother and in the end his Mummy decided there was only one thing for it—she'd have to sell him. So she took him to the shop and the lady paid a pound for him and put him on the shelf in between the tins of cat food and the Weetabix. And there the little boy stood all day. And all day people walked past and looked at him and said things like, 'One pound for that little boy! He doesn't look worth it to me.' 'He looks

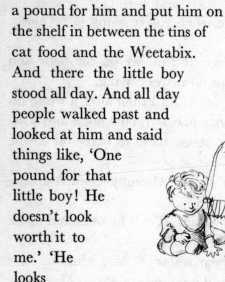

rather a rough boy,' said one little girl. A baby going past in a pram just locked at him and burst into tears. One lady said, 'He looks a greedy little boy to me. I don't think I want *him*.' And so all day long the little boy stood on the shelf while strange people walked by saying nasty things about him. And at night the shop closed and the boy was all alone.

"And the next morning it started all over again. The strange people walking past and saying that they didn't like the look of the little boy. Until suddenly along came somebody the little boy *did* know. It was his Mummy with his baby brother in the pram. And as his Mummy stopped to pick up cat food his little brother saw him and smiled and reached his arms to him. And then his mother saw him too and her eyes lit up and she said, 'Ah! what a lovely looking boy! Just what I want. Just the sort of little boy I'd like to have.' And she took the little boy off the shelf and bought him and took him home and the boy was ever so happy again. There — did you like that story, Wallace?"

"I did," said Wallace. "Mummy, can I have my ice lolly now?"

"Yes, Wallace," said Mummy, smiling. "You can have your ice lolly." And she got it for him.

Cleaning the Windows

One afternoon Wallace's Daddy was making wine in the kitchen. Mummy was resting upstairs.

"Can I help, Daddy?" said Wallace.

"All right," said Daddy.

Wallace pulled up a chair to stand on and looked at Daddy's collection of bottles and jars and tubes and corks. Daddy gave him a plastic jug of water and Wallace poured it into one of the big jars. "This is ginger beer," he said. Only it didn't all go in; a lot of it spilled.

"I think that's enough of that," said Daddy. He wiped up the water with a cloth. "Perhaps you'd better leave this to me, Wallace," he said. "Go and play with your toys, eh?"

"All right," said Wallace, and he went off and made a traffic jam on the window sill in the dining-room. When he looked out of the windows he saw how dirty they were. He went into the kitchen to tell Daddy.

"Of course they're dirty," said Daddy. "You've breathed on them and then drawn on them. You've stuck plasticine and sticky paper on them.

"*And* I squashed a fly on them," said Wallace.

"No wonder they're dirty," said Daddy.

"Shall I clean them then?" Wallace asked.

"Good idea," said Daddy.

"Will you give me a bucketful of things to clean them with?" asked Wallace.

"Oh! all right." Daddy was very busy with his wine.

He got a bucket and filled it with warm water.

"*And* some bubbles," said Wallace.

Daddy put the bubbles in. Wallace put on his boots and his red apron with the soldier on the front.

"I'm ready," he said. "Bring the bucket, Daddy."

"Take the bucket yourself," said Daddy. "Show what a big boy you are."

Wallace carried the bucket through to the dining-room. He spilt a bit on the way. Then he set to work to clean the windows.

It was difficult. There was so much water in the cloth and it dripped everywhere, not just over the window but on to the window sill too. It dripped on to the radiator and down on to the lino. It went all over the toy chest and into many of Wallace's cars. It also ran up his arms. Wallace went into the kitchen.

"Will you roll up my sleeves, Daddy?" he asked.

"Roll them yourself," said Daddy.

"And I need a brush," said Wallace.

"Then find one and stop pestering me." Daddy was cross.

Wallace found a brush in the box with the shoe polish in. But it was no good for cleaning windows.

"I need a drying-up cloth, Daddy," Wallace said. Daddy threw one at him. Wallace began to dry the windows. He dried the sill and he dried the toy box. But as he was getting off the toy box he knocked the

bucket over—SPLOOSH—it rushed bubbly water all over the lino and even onto the carpet.

"Oh! *what* have you done, Wallace?" said Daddy. He came in and saw the water all over the floor. "Oh no! Oh Wallace! Really! You *are* clumsy. Go and get the mop. I suppose *I'll* have to clear up."

Wallace went and got the broom.

"Not a broom, Wallace," said Daddy. "A *mop*. Oh! just go away, will you? You'll only make things worse. Go on. Out!"

Wallace went into the sitting-room and looked out of the window. He could hear Daddy squeezing water and clattering the mop about. Then Daddy went back into the kitchen but Wallace didn't come out. He stayed in the sitting-room, breathing on the windows and drawing on them.

Then suddenly there was a terrible crash from the kitchen. Daddy shouted something loudly. Wallace went running along to see what had happened. One of the huge jars was broken on the floor. There was glass and wine everywhere and a strong smell of wine.

"Did you knock it over?" asked Wallace.

"Yes, I did," said Daddy angrily, and he started picking up the pieces.

"Never mind," said Wallace. "I'll help."

"No. You stay away," said Daddy.

Then Mummy came downstairs.

"Gracious!" she said. "What a mess!"

"Blasted thing slipped," said Daddy.

"Oh no!" said Mummy. "You *are* clumsy."

"It's all right," said Daddy. "I'll clear it up."

"No. You'll only make things worse," said Mummy. "Messing up my kitchen. Just go away, will you. Go on—out! Both of you!"

Daddy and Wallace left the kitchen and went into the sitting-room.

"I've been breathing on *these* windows, Daddy," said Wallace. "*And* drawing on them. Aren't they dirty?"

"Yes they are—very dirty," Daddy agreed.

"Shall we clean them, Daddy?" said Wallace.

"No," said Daddy. "No more cleaning and no more making a mess with water, eh? I'll tell you what we'll do. We'll *both* breathe on them and draw some more pictures, shall we?"

"That's a good idea," said Wallace.

So that's what they did.

The New House

One day they were driving in the car. Wallace was looking at the pictures in his Dinky catalogue. He said, "Where are we going?"

"We're going to look at a house," said Mummy. "It's going to be our new house."

"But I like it at home," said Wallace. "Ooh! Look, Dad—Range-Rover, Police Range-Rover. That's my favourite."

"Perhaps you'll get one for your birthday," said Dad.

There was no one living in their new house. There weren't even any chairs or curtains. It was empty and cold.

"Do you like this house, Wallace?" said Daddy.

"No," said Wallace.

Mum and Dad went round looking at things although there was nothing to look at. Dad had his tape measure.

"Go into the garden, Wallace, and see what you can find," said Dad. But Wallace didn't want to go by himself.

"This is your room, Wallace," said Mum. "Look, here's a cupboard all of your own." Wallace opened the door. "Here you can hang your party suit and your

Paddington coat. You can put your socks up here. And your shoes can go under there."

"That's nice," said Wallace. "Will my bunk bed go in this room?"

"Yes—just there," said Mum.

"Let's go outside now," said Wallace. But there was no sandpit outside and nothing to play with.

"We've brought your tricycle, Wallace," said Mum.

"It's too bumpy here," said Wallace. Then he found a bicycle tyre in the grass.

"Look at this, Dad. I could throw this."

"You could hang it from the apple tree," said Mum, "and swing from it."

"That's a good idea," said Wallace.

Daddy hung the tyre up with a piece of old washing line. Wallace climbed into the tyre and swung round and round. That was good.

"Look at me," he shouted.

Then the rope slipped and he fell to the ground.

"I want to go home," he said.

"We will soon," Daddy replied. He was weeding the rhubarb.

Then Wallace came across a tree on the edge of the lawn. "I can climb this tree," he said, and he clambered about like a monkey.

"We could call that *your* tree," said Dad.

Then Wallace saw something in the flower bed.

"Look what I've found, Dad." And he showed Daddy the toy half covered in earth. "It's a Range-Rover, isn't it, Dad?" They washed it in the water tub.

"No, just a Land-Rover," Daddy replied. Most of the paint had come off and it had no tyres.

"I *do* want a Range-Rover," said Wallace.

"I know," said Dad. "Come and collect worms with me."

Wallace found a great metal tub near the rhubarb. There was a little water in the bottom of it. Wallace dropped some stones in, then a worm. "Hey, Dad! I could make a stew," said Wallace.

"Good idea," Daddy replied.

And Wallace put in some gravel, a few handfuls of grass, some dandelions, a crisp packet and some little apples that had fallen off the tree. Then he stirred it all round with a bit of bamboo.

"What shall I do now, Dad?" he asked.

"We're going home now," said Dad.

"Good," said Wallace.

On the way home Mummy asked him, "Would you like to go and live there?"

"No," said Wallace.

But they went to visit the house again a few days later. When they arrived Wallace wouldn't get out but sat in the car looking at his Dinky catalogue. After a while Mummy came and said, "Wallace, I think there might be a suprise for you in your room."

Wallace ran into the house. But he couldn't see anything in his room at all. "Look in your cupboard," said Mum. Wallace looked and there was a Range-Rover: a Police Range-Rover, white with a blue and red stripe down the side. The back doors opened and there were two little stand-up signs saying, "Police: Slow". The Range-Rover ran very well on the bare floorboards of his empty room.

Soon Daddy said, "Time to go, Wallace."

Wallace said, "I don't want to go," but Mummy said, "Biscuits," and Wallace went downstairs. He was just about to get into the car when he suddenly remembered. "Dad, let's go and look at my stew."

"All right," said Daddy, "but quickly."

The stew was getting on very nicely. All the grass and stuff had come to the top in a thick scum. Wallace gave it a good stir.

"Come on now," said Dad.

"I want to climb in my tree," said Wallace.

"No time," Daddy replied and bundled Wallace into the car.

"Daddy wouldn't let me climb in the tree, Mum," said Wallace. He was nearly crying.

"Next time," said Mum and gave him two ginger biscuits.·

Wallace munched them as they drove off. Then Mum said, "Hey, Wallace. When we live in our new house you can climb in your tree *every day*."

"Every day?" asked Wallace.

"Yes," said Mummy, "every day. Just think of that."

So Wallace sat back with his Range-Rover and just thought of that.

Helping the Birds

One day when Daddy and Wallace and Henry came down for breakfast they found little brown feathers scattered over the kitchen floor.

"Oh no!" said Wallace. "Wussy's had a bird again, Dad."

"That's the second this week," said Dad. "D you remember the sparrow he got when the builders were relining the roof?"

"Yes," said Wallace, "and he got a mouse once."

"He had a baby rabbit in here the other night too, don't tell Mummy," said Dad.

"*And* he nearly got those jerbils that came to stay." said Wallace. "Let's not give him any breakfast, Dad."

"If we don't, he'll only catch more birds and things," Dad replied and he gave Wussy his plate of meat. "Anyway it's his nature to catch things—like a lion catching a zebra."

"I don't like you, Wussy," said Wallace and baby Henry came and hit Wussy with his tractor.

That very same day Wallace came out of the front door and there was Wussy with a little bird in his mouth. Wallace shouted and stamped at Wussy and he ran away. The little bird stayed where it was, cowering on the doorstep.

"Naughty Wussy," said Wallace. "Is it hurt, Dad?"

"Doesn't seem to be," Daddy replied. But the little bird just sat there with its bright startled eyes.

"Shall we look after it, Dad?" said Wallace.

"If we don't Wussy will only get it again," Daddy replied, "or it'll die of cold." And he picked up the little bird in his hands.

"Is it a sparrow, Dad?" asked Wallace.

"No, I think it's a female robin," Daddy replied.

Then they got a cardboard box and Wallace put some twigs and fluffy dried grass in it for a nest. They brought a little ash-tray for water and they gave it some peanuts, a cheese biscuit, the remains of Henry's apple, half a Weetabix and some bread. They also dug up two worms, a big one and a little one.

"Well, he's bound to like *something* there," said Dad. They watched to see what the bird would do but it wouldn't do anything. It had hopped into a corner and there it sat. They could see its body moving up and down with the beating of its heart.

"He's had a bad shock," said Dad. "Let's leave him be."

They put wire-netting over the top to keep Wussy out.

At bed-time Wallace looked in again but the little bird still hadn't moved.

"Wussy didn't hurt him badly, did he?" Wallace asked.

"We'll see in the morning," said Dad.

But in the morning the bird was dead, lying on the bottom of the box beside his water-tray. They buried him under Wallace's apple tree.

At breakfast they could see Wussy crouching at his
special pouncing place on the other side of the lawn.

"Wussy's catching more mice, Dad," said Wallace.
"I think we should get rid of him."

"Well," said Daddy, "if we didn't have Wussy we'd
have mice doing droppings under the sink and eating
the bottom out of the porridge oats sack. He does a good
job for us."

"But he needn't catch birds too," said Wallace.
"*They* don't do any harm."

"They do to my vegetables," said Dad, "but I suppose
as it's winter there are no vegetables for them to eat."

"Let's put some food out for them, Dad," said Wallace.

"They can have my bread." And he threw it out of the back door.

"Wussy will pounce on them if they come close to the house," said Daddy. "I know. Didn't someone give you a bird-feeder thing for Christmas? Let's find that."

The bird-feeder was a coil of wire to put food in and it had a sucker to stick it on the window. Wallace crammed his bread into it and they stuck it on to the kitchen window so that they could see the birds feeding as they had breakfast. But no birds came, even though it was frosty and Daddy said they had nothing to eat. The bread went mouldy.

"It's no good," said Dad. "It's too near the house. They're frightened to come so close."

"Yes, they're frightened of Wussy," said Wallace.

"We'll just have to build a bird table—that's all," said Dad.

"Oh yes!" said Wallace. "We'll need a hammer and some nails and a bit of wood for the bottom and a bit for the sides and it must have a roof with a hole for the birds to go in and . . ."

"Just a simple table," said Daddy. "Not a nesting box."

So they found a bit of sawn-off branch for a post, rather bent but long. "It must be high, you see," said Dad. "Otherwise Wussy will jump up to it."

64

They thumped the post into the ground in the middle of the lawn. "Now the top," said Dad.

"But it should be square," said Wallace.

"Well, I'm afraid it's triangular," said Daddy, and he hammered it onto the post with one nail. "There," he said, "now for some food."

Mummy had got some strips of pork fat on a string so they hung that off one corner of the table and put some breadcrumbs on top.

Then they went inside to watch. In no time at all a pair of blue tits came and hung upside down on the fat to peck at it.

"Oh! Dad, look!" Wallace cried out. "Here comes Wussy. He'll catch them!"

But the birds flew away long before Wussy got near them. "They can see him coming across the lawn," said Daddy. "And anyway they're so high up Wussy can't reach them."

They watched Wussy jumping up on his hind legs to bat at the string of fat spinning in the air. But he couldn't reach it.

"Ha! ha!" said Wallace. "That's fixed him, Dad."

Wussy wandered slowly away and the birds came back.

The next morning at breakfast they watched the blue tits on the fat and the sparrows and starlings fighting over the bread.

"Wussy can't get them, can he, Dad?" said Wallace. "I wonder where he is." Then he saw him. He was crouched at his pouncing place, very still except for his tail which was swishing from side to side.

"Oh dear!" said Wallace. "Wussy can still catch the mice, can't he, Dad?"

"Yes, I'm afraid he can, and he will," said Dad. "But we have done something for the birds, Wallace, and we can't save everything."

An Afternoon Surprise

After lunch one day Wallace switched off the telly and said, "I think I'll be a fireman when I grow up. Wake up, Daddy. What shall we do now?"

Daddy opened his eyes and said, "I thought we might make bread this afternoon."

"Oh no!" said Wallace, "that's boring."

"All right, we'll go out then," said Dad.

"To the playground?" asked Wallace.

"We went there yesterday," Daddy replied. "Why don't you play in the sandpit while I dig the garden."

"I want to stay inside," said Wallace.

"Well, we're going out. Shall we go to the lake?"

"That's too far," said Wallace.

"We'll go up to the end of the village and post the letters then," said Dad. "You can push the push-chair if you like."

"I don't want to go," said Wallace.

"Bad luck because we're going," said Dad. "But when we come back, you can have some orange and a biscuit and I'll play you beggar-my-neighbour."

"Oh! all right," said Wallace and he put his boots on while Daddy got his brother Henry up from his rest.

"I'm cold," Wallace said as they trudged up the hill.

"Then walk faster," Daddy replied.

"It's so boring," said Wallace. "Dad, can't we go to the playground?"

"No. Now don't whine. You never know, something interesting might happen."

When they got to the post box Wallace posted the letters. They were about to go home when Daddy said, "Look, there's a breakdown lorry in front of the garage."

"To-jo, you mean," said Wallace. "Shall we go and have a look?"

"All right," said Dad.

"It's a Land-Rover really, isn't it?" Wallace said when they got up to it. It was painted blue and yellow but the paint was coming off and it was a bit rusty.

"It looks very old," said Wallace.

"Her name's Bertha," came a strange voice, "and she's towed more wrecks than you've had hot dinners." A man with a spanner wriggled out from underneath the to-jo. He had a hat on with furry flaps to keep his ears warm. "And she isn't dead yet," said the man, "for all she's done going on a hundred thousand miles on her second engine. Want to get up there?"

"Yes please," said Wallace and the man hoisted him up on to the back so that he stood beside the lifting arm and the winch. On the floor there was a lot of oil and some chain.

The man said to Wallace, "Perhaps one day you'll be here when we have to go out on a pick-up—then you could come too. Would you like that?"

"Ooh! Yes please," said Wallace.

"Good," said the man. "See you some time then."

"Cheerio," said Wallace and they left the garage and started walking home.

"Can we go there again tomorrow, Dad?" said Wallace. "I *would* like to go out in Bertha."

"Perhaps one day you will," said Daddy.

"I hope it'll be soon," said Wallace.

It was sooner than they expected. They were just getting near home when there was a squeal of brakes in the road beside them and there was Bertha. The man from the garage leant across and said through the window, "Coming then?"

"Yes please," Daddy replied and they all climbed into the front. They put Henry's push-chair into the back with the chains and Daddy held Henry on his knees and Wallace sat next to the driver. Wallace didn't usually sit in the front of cars and it was exciting but a bit frightening because there was a little hole in the floor at his feet and he could see the road going by underneath. There was a terrible smell of petrol.

"Somebody broken down?" Daddy asked the man.

The man laughed and shook his head so that the furry flaps to his hat flopped about like a dog's ears. "More like broken *in*, by the sound of it," he said. "See in a minute."

And soon they had stopped.

"Good Lord!" exclaimed Daddy. "I always thought this was a dangerous corner. Anybody hurt?"

"No," said the man, "just a lot of damage."

"What is it?" asked Wallace and then he saw. The house on the corner had a car sticking out of it. There was glass and bricks everywhere.

"Took the corner too fast," said the driver, "went

through the garden wall, through the window and ended up on the front room carpet."

Wallace saw his friend the builder there with his van. He was taking out some scaffolding poles and putting them up in the wall of the house.

"The car's almost knocked the house down," Daddy explained, "and now it's holding the house *up*. If they took the car away without those poles, it probably *would* fall down."

"Ready then," said the builder after a while and Bertha's driver slowly backed her towards the car. She bumped over the remains of the wall and her rear wheels sank into the flower-bed. Wallace watched through the back window of the cab as the driver clanked about with chain on the back and then fixed Bertha's hook on to something underneath the car's boot. Next he took a great handle and turned the winch until the back wheels of the car were well off the ground. Then he got up into the cab again. "Tricky part, this," he said, putting Bertha into gear. "Hold on tight."

Wallace clung on to the seat and continued watching through the back window as the driver revved up the engine. They began to move slowly forward. There was a jerk as the chain took the strain of the car, Bertha's engine roared some more and there was a bump as she bounced over the broken-down wall and the car was dragged out of the house, bricks and dust and some window frame crashing down on to the ground as it went.

When Bertha had pulled the car out on to the road, Wallace and Daddy and Henry thanked the driver and got out. Before setting off for home they looked at the house. They could see right into the front room. It was a terrible sight: the telly fallen on to its screen, a little table smashed and an armchair full of bricks. The builder was looking in too and shaking his head slowly from side to side.

They watched while Bertha hitched up the front of the car instead of the back and drove off slowly towards the garage. Wallace waved to the man with the ear-flaps and they set off home again.

"That was good, wasn't it, Wallace?" said Dad.

"Yes," said Wallace.

"You see—I was right," said Dad, "something interesting *did* happen."

"Yes," said Wallace. "Dad, do you know what I want to be when I grow up?"

"A fireman."

"No," said Wallace.

"What then?"

"A breakdown driver," said Wallace. "That's what I want to be."

Wallace Says Thank You

"Granny's coming this afternoon," said Mummy one day.

"Oh good!" said Wallace. "She always brings me something."

"Yes, but it's her birthday tomorrow. *You* must give *her* something."

"Perhaps I could give her a bowl like I gave you, Mum."

"Rather expensive," said Mum.

"*I* know!" said Wallace. "I could give her something for me to play with when I'm staying there."

"Not much fun for her," said Mum. "Come on, let's go down to the shops and see what we can find."

They bought a box of chocolates.

"We've forgotten a card," Mum said on the way back.

"Playschool" on the telly was about donkeys so Wallace did a picture of a donkey. And a soldier.

When Granny came Wallace said, "Have you got something for me?"

Granny gave him a red and yellow tipper-truck.

"What do you say?" said Mummy. But Wallace was looking at the tipper-truck. "Wallace, what do you say?"

"Thank you," said Wallace very quietly.

Then Granny read Wallace's comic to him and mended his slipper while they watched the telly.

"Let's play in my sandpit now, Granny," said Wallace. Wallace took his new tipper-truck with him.

"You don't want to get that dirty already, do you?" said Mum.

Then he began to get rather rough, throwing sand about, and by mistake hit Granny above the eye with his spade. When they played football Wallace kicked the ball into the roses and made Granny get it. Then he started pulling at her and interrupting when she was talking to Mummy.

When Granny left, Wallace wouldn't give her the card and the present he had got for her and Mummy had to give them. And he wouldn't say goodbye or thank you for the tipper-truck. And Mummy was very angry when he wouldn't get it in from the sandpit at bath time. "You don't deserve it," she said.

In the morning Wallace felt sick. And hot. And his legs felt very tired. Mummy put her hand on his forehead and took his temperature.

"Mmm," she said. "Would you like some breakfast?"

"No, thank you," said Wallace in a weak voice.

But he had to get up to go and see the doctor. On the way he met James going to playgroup. "I'm not coming today," said Wallace. "I'm ill."

They had to wait a long time in the doctor's waiting-room and Mummy read him three books. But in the end they saw the doctor. He put his cold stethoscope on Wallace's front and back and looked down his throat. On the way out they collected some medicine:

a raspberry-coloured one and a pink one to keep in the fridge.

When they got back home Wallace felt perfectly all right and had a good play of the game on the back of the Weetabix packet. He beat Mummy twice.

Then he felt very cold and weak again so he went back to bed with some hot Ribena and Mummy put his records on for him.

"Anything else you want?" she said.

"I'd like my tipper-truck please," said Wallace.

"You left it in the sandpit," said Mummy.

"Will you get it for me?" Wallace asked.

"I didn't think you cared about it—leaving it there," said Mummy.

"I *do* care," said Wallace.

In a few minutes Mummy came back with it.

"It's all dirty," said Wallace.

"Well, you know why, don't you?" said Mum.

"But will you clean it?"

Mummy didn't look very pleased but she did clean it and Wallace lay down with his nice new tipper-truck and fell asleep.

When he woke up again he felt much better and went downstairs.

"How are you feeling?" asked Mum.

"All right," said Wallace but his voice had gone and all that came out was a whisper. Mummy and Wallace both laughed.

"Well, what do you feel like doing now?" Mummy asked.

"I think I'll draw a picture for Granny," Wallace whispered, "because it's her birthday today."

So he sat down and drew a picture of a castle with a soldier.

"Why, Wallace!" Mummy exclaimed. "I think that's the best drawing you've ever done."

"Shall I write something too?" Wallace whispered.

Mummy wrote a message for Wallace to copy. "Dear Granny, thank you for my tipper-truck. Love Wallace." Wallace wrote all those words out himself.

"Well done, Wallace." said Mum. "Do you know I think that's the best bit of *writing* you've ever done."

"Now you do the envelope, Mum," whispered Wallace. Mum did that and said, "Now you've given her a present and a card and a picture and a thank-you letter—all that for her birthday."

"Yes," said Wallace, still whispering, "and I expect Granny *will* be pleased."

Jeff Brown

FLAT STANLEY

Stanley Lambchop is just a normal healthy boy, though since a large notice-board fell on him, he's been only half an inch thick!

For Stanley this presents no problems, in fact he finds he can do all sorts of things and go to places never before possible.

Jeff Brown's hilarious text and Tomi Ungerer's equally funny drawings make this book absolutely irresistible.

Anne Fine

BILL'S NEW FROCK

When Bill Simpson woke up on Monday morning, he found he was a girl . . . Forced off to school in a frilly, pink dress, Bill discovers one of the worst days of his life is about to begin . . .

Baffled by the way things are just *different* for girls, Bill falls headlong into trouble. As the amazing day drags on Bill's new frock becomes dirtier and tattier. How will it all end for him – or her?

Winner of The Smarties Award

Margaret Greaves

CHARLIE, EMMA AND ALBERIC

Charlie and Emma want a pet of their own. Then one day they find a tiny dragon. Of course, Alberic wants to go home with them – and that's when their adventures start!

The first story of Charlie, Emma and their magic dragon.

Also available

Charlie, Emma and the Dragon Family
Charlie, Emma and the School Dragon
Charlie, Emma and Dragons to the Rescue
Charlie, Emma and the Juggling Dragon

A Selected List of Fiction from Mammoth

While every effort is made to keep prices low, it is sometimes necessary to increase prices at short notice. Mammoth Books reserves the right to show new retail prices on covers which may differ from those previously advertised in the text or elsewhere.

The prices shown below were correct at the time of going to press.

☐	7497 0366 0	**Dilly the Dinosaur**	Tony Bradman	£1.99
☐	7497 0021 1	**Dilly and the Tiger**	Tony Bradman	£1.99
☐	7497 0137 4	**Flat Stanley**	Jeff Brown	£1.99
☐	7497 0048 3	**Friends and Brothers**	Dick King-Smith	£1.99
☐	7497 0054 8	**My Naughty Little Sister**	Dorothy Edwards	£1.99
☐	416 86550 X	**Cat Who Wanted to go Home**	Jill Tomlinson	£1.99
☐	7497 0166 8	**The Witch's Big Toe**	Ralph Wright	£1.99
☐	7497 0218 4	**Lucy Jane at the Ballet**	Susan Hampshire	£2.25
☐	416 03212 5	**I Don't Want To!**	Bel Mooney	£1.99
☐	7497 0030 0	**I Can't Find It!**	Bel Mooney	£1.99
☐	7497 0032 7	**The Bear Who Stood on His Head**	W. J. Corbett	£1.99
☐	416 10362 6	**Owl and Billy**	Martin Waddell	£1.75
☐	416 13822 5	**It's Abigail Again**	Moira Miller	£1.75
☐	7497 0031 9	**King Tubbitum and the Little Cook**	Margaret Ryan	£1.99
☐	7497 0041 6	**The Quiet Pirate**	Andrew Matthews	£1.99
☐	7497 0064 5	**Grump and the Hairy Mammoth**	Derek Sampson	£1.99

All these books are available at your bookshop or newsagent, or can be ordered direct from the publisher. Just tick the titles you want and fill in the form below.

Mandarin Paperbacks, Cash Sales Department, PO Box 11, Falmouth, Cornwall TR10 9EN.

Please send cheque or postal order, no currency, for purchase price quoted and allow the following for postage and packing:

UK	80p for the first book, 20p for each additional book ordered to a maximum charge of £2.00.
BFPO	80p for the first book, 20p for each additional book.
Overseas including Eire	£1.50 for the first book, £1.00 for the second and 30p for each additional book thereafter.

NAME (Block letters) ....

ADDRESS ....

....

....